Aberdeenshire
COUNCIL

Aberdeenshire Libraries
www.aberdeenshire.gov.uk/libraries
Renewals Hotline 01224 661511

Raintree is an imprint of Capstone Global Library Limited,
a company incorporated in England and Wales having its
registered office at 7 Pilgrim Street, London, EC4V 6LB –
Registered company number: 6695582

To contact Raintree, please email myorders@raintreepublishers.co.uk.

First published in Australia by Black Dog Books in 2007
Copyright © Bernadette Kelly 2007
First published in the United Kingdom in 2013
The moral rights of the proprietor have been asserted.

Editor: Laura Knowles
Art Director: Kay Fraser
Graphic Designer: Emily Harris
Production Specialist: Michelle Biedscheid
Originated by Capstone Global Library Ltd
Printed and bound in China

Main cover photograph reproduced with permission
of Shutterstock/© Judy Drietz. Background image reproduced
with permission of Shutterstock/© Andrew Zarivny.

ISBN 978 1 406 26675 7 (paperback)
17 16 15 14 13
10 9 8 7 6 5 4 3 2 1

British Library Cataloguing in Publication Data
A full catalogue record for this book is available from the British Library.

Taking a Break

Bernadette Kelly

I leaned over the saddle and held out my
hand. My eyes stayed glued on Matt Snyder,
thundering towards me on his Appaloosa horse,
Bullet.

My own horse, Bobby, fidgeted beneath me.
Matt charged by, passing the wooden baton into
my waiting hand.

My fingers closed over the baton. At the same
time, I nudged Bobby forward with my legs.

"Go, Annie!" yelled Matt.

I barely heard the shouts of my teammates, and I didn't notice the opposing team in the next lane. As my team's final rider in the relay, it was my job to keep the lead that the others had gained.

All I had to do was weave my horse through the bending poles, turn, and gallop back to pass the finish line. We were way ahead, and it should have been an easy win. But something was wrong with Bobby. He didn't seem to want to move. He broke into an unenthusiastic trot.

I used my legs to give Bobby the message to canter.

"Come on, Bobby, go," I whispered. I squeezed my legs on his sides again.

Bobby's ears were flat against his head. He trotted faster for a stride or two, and then slowed down. I had to push again or he would have fallen back into a walk.

I glanced nervously across to the rider in the next lane. It was Austin Ryan on his big Thoroughbred mare, Cruise.

Austin wasn't much of a games rider. He preferred eventing and had only joined the race because we needed to have an equal number of riders on both teams. But even though he didn't like riding in games, Austin was quickly gaining ground on me now.

Desperate to stay ahead of Austin, I kept going. I kicked furiously at the sides of my reluctant horse.

Bobby dropped his head and lifted his back legs in a half-hearted buck, almost unseating me. Even though I was concentrating on the race, I started to feel a little worried. Bobby had never done that before.

By the time I finally crossed the finish line, Austin's team was already celebrating. My teammates – Matt, Bryce, and Natalie – were staring at me. My team had been leading for most of the relay.

No one was happy that we'd lost.

"I'm sorry," I mumbled.

Natalie and Bryce didn't say anything, but I could see how disappointed they were.

"Good thing we were racing against our own club members and not at an official competition," said Matt, shrugging.

I looked gratefully at Matt. I'd expected him to be upset about losing. He was the most competitive games rider at Ridgeview Riding Club. But he was right, of course. We weren't in a real competition. Thank goodness.

Today was the last riding club event for the year. Mrs Mason, the club's district commissioner, had split everybody out of our usual groups for the games. She had mixed up the junior and senior riders, as well as my own group, the intermediates. We were all riding against people from our own riding club. In a real competition, we'd ride against riders at our own level from other clubs.

After I unsaddled Bobby and put him back in his paddock with a supply of hay and fresh water, I made my way to the riding club's lunch shed to order some lunch.

After I picked up my cheese toastie, I looked around until I found Reese Moriarty. My friend and next-door neighbour was sitting at a table with Matt, Austin, and Jessica Coulson – all members of my usual group. Like me, they all wore the Ridgeview Riding Club uniform.

I would have liked to talk to Reese, but I didn't think I was ready to face the others.

Austin would probably be quietly smug about beating me, and Jessica would probably say something mean about Bobby or even about my riding.

No. I didn't feel like dealing with them. Instead, I made my way outside with my lunch. I hadn't taken more than a few steps out of the shed when a familiar voice said, "Is there something wrong with our company?" It was Reese. She had followed me outside.

"No. It's not that," I said. I sighed.

As we walked, Reese finished the last mouthful of her hot dog. We headed to a grassy patch away from the lunch shed. We sat down, resting our backs against a tall tree.

"The groups are back to normal after lunch," Reese said. She yawned. "We have a dressage lesson with Erica. I feel tired just thinking about it. Here, want some?" she added, handing me a chocolate bar.

"I think Bobby needs the energy more than I do," I said, breaking off a chunk of the chocolate bar and handing the rest back to Reese. "He was awful today. He tried to buck me off."

"You're kidding! Bobby never does stuff like that," Reese said.

I nodded. "I know," I said. "It was really weird." I picked at a tuft of grass. Frowning, I yanked up a green blade and began tearing it in half.

"Maybe you should talk to Erica about it," Reese said.

Erica was the riding club dressage instructor. She was also the owner of a riding school and training stable in Ridgeview. I worked there part-time, after school and when I had time on weekends, and during the summer.

I had landed my job soon after moving to the town. I still couldn't believe Erica had hired me. I didn't know anything about horses back then. I'd always loved them, but it was only since moving to Ridgeview that I had the chance to ride and own my own horse.

Reese was right. If anybody could tell me what was wrong with Bobby, it would be Erica.

"What time is it?" I asked.

Reese checked her mobile. "We still have half an hour for lunch break," said Reese.

I stood up. "Well, I can't wait that long," I said. "Something's wrong with Bobby, and I need to find out what it is – now!"

Chapter Two

I found Erica eating her lunch at the instructors' table. I explained my concerns about Bobby, and Erica listened patiently.

"Sounds like he needs a break from riding," she said as soon as I'd finished telling her about Bobby.

I looked blankly at her. I loved riding Bobby, and I did it as often as I could, every weekend and as many nights after school as my homework load would allow.

"Why?" I asked.

Erica sighed. "Think about it, Annie. You get school holidays, don't you?" she asked.

I nodded.

Erica went on, "And people who work for a living get holiday time. Even the riding club has a break over the hottest part of summer. We all need a break from time to time, so why should horses be any different?"

"That makes sense, I guess," I said quietly. "But what does that mean?"

Erica looked at me and said, "I think Bobby's grumpy behaviour is because he's tired, Annie. He just needs a break."

My face fell. "But I thought Bobby liked being ridden," I said quietly.

"It's not the end of the world," Erica said, giving me a small smile. "Most horses come back better than ever after they have a little bit of time off. I'm sure you can find something else to do for a few weeks."

I nodded. "If it's all right with you, I don't think I'll come to the dressage lesson. I think I'll start Bobby's break right now." I paused. "Well, I still have to ride him home," I added.

Erica smiled. "That won't hurt him," she said. "But if you're not riding this afternoon, just let Mrs Mason know. She'll probably find you something else to do to help out."

When I told Mrs Mason I wouldn't be riding for the rest of the day, she immediately sent me to the show-jumping area. For the next two sessions, Bobby rested while I lifted jump rails whenever a horse or rider knocked them down.

Reese and I rode home that afternoon on a trail that wound through the national forest on the edge of Ridgeview.

The two horses stayed close together, walking at the same speed. Jefferson's grey coat contrasted with Bobby's reddish colouring.

As we ambled along, I told Reese what Erica had said about Bobby taking a break.

"That makes sense," Reese said. "Erica is usually right about that kind of thing. And it would explain Bobby's behaviour today."

"I know," I said with a sigh. "I'm still sad about it, though."

We stopped at my house's gate to say goodbye. "Well, I guess we won't be riding together over the Easter holidays," I said, sighing. "There go my plans for having a good time while we're off school."

I grabbed a thick hunk of Bobby's mane and ran my fingers through it. Then I said, "I've never seen you give Jefferson a break, Reese. How come he doesn't need one?"

"Actually, he does, every year," said Reese.

My eyes widened. "He does? When?" I asked.

"Don't you remember? Mum and I visit my grandmother for three weeks every summer," Reese said.

"Oh yeah," I said. "How could I forget? After all, I horse-sat Jefferson last year." I paused and added, "I wish I could visit someone, or go on a trip or something. I don't know how I'll make it. How will I stay busy?"

"You only have to rest him for a couple of weeks," Reese said.

She gathered up her reins and turned Jefferson back to the road. "It's not that long," she added. "You'll find something to do. See ya later." Reese waved before riding on to her own house next door.

* * *

After dinner that evening, my parents curled up on the sofa to watch a detective show on TV. It didn't take long before I was bored. I was thinking about going to bed early when the phone rang.

"Can you get that, Annie?" my mum asked.

"Sure," I said, getting off the couch. I ran into the kitchen to pick up the phone.

"Annie, it's me," a familiar voice said.

I squealed with delight at the sound of my friend's voice. "Jade!" I said happily.

Jade O'Brien and I had once been inseparable. But that was in the city. Then my family had moved to Ridgeview and everything had changed. I now had a whole new set of friends, but I still kept in touch with Jade. She reminded me of my old life. I missed it, even though I loved my new life in Ridgeview.

"So what's new?" I asked.

Jade's world was shopping and going to the cinema – far removed from my calmer life in the country.

"Oh, you know, same old stuff," said Jade. "Dave has a new girlfriend. She's okay, but I know Dave, so I bet she won't be around for too long."

I laughed. Dave was Jade's older brother. He always had a new girlfriend. He collected girls like I collected horse magazines.

"So what are your plans for the holidays?" asked Jade.

I shrugged. "Not sure," I said. "I don't really have anything planned yet."

"Good!" Jade said. "Next weekend I'm coming to your place."

"You are?" I asked. I brightened. Hanging out with Jade for a few days would take my mind off not riding.

"Yep. I mean, if your parents don't mind, of course," Jade added hastily.

I laughed. "Of course they won't!" I said. My parents loved Jade, and they had felt guilty about taking me away from her. They wanted to make sure we stayed friends.

"You can teach me how to ride Bobby while I'm there," said Jade. "I bet by the end of the trip I'll be riding as well as you do."

I took a deep breath. "Oh. Um . . . I don't think –" I began.

"Don't worry, I promise not to hurt your precious horse," interrupted Jade. "Besides, you'll be there to teach me."

I tried to let Jade down gently. "I can't let you ride Bobby, Jade. I'm sorry. Not this time," I said slowly.

"But I really want to learn to ride," said Jade, confusion creeping into her voice. "What's the matter, don't you trust me with him?" she asked. "Or is he hurt or something?"

"Not exactly. And it's not that I don't trust you. Don't worry. I'll explain when you get here," I promised.

"Well, you'd better have a good reason, Annie Boyd," Jade said, sounding a little annoyed. "Got to go, but I'll see you on Friday night."

"Bye," I said.

After we hung up, I stared at the phone, wondering what to do. Jade had sounded really disappointed when I said I couldn't let her ride Bobby.

But what could I do about it? For one thing, I knew for a fact that nobody learned to ride in just a few days. Not well, anyway. I'd learned that the hard way.

And I couldn't change my mind about giving Bobby a rest. I had to do the right thing for my horse, no matter what other people wanted. Even my best friend.

But Jade was going to be here next weekend. I really wanted my time with Jade to be fun for both of us.

I thought about asking Reese if Jade could ride Jefferson. But Jade and Reese didn't really get along, and I didn't want to risk it.

I sighed. There wasn't a way to give Bobby a rest and teach Jade to ride. Not at the same time, anyway.

Chapter
Three

I couldn't fall asleep that night. Jade's visit and Bobby's behaviour kept my thoughts busy.

Jade had been to visit me before, but she had never asked to ride Bobby. Any other time, I would have been more than happy to teach her how to ride. But the way my horse had been behaving lately, it could be dangerous to let a complete beginner on his back.

If Bobby tried to throw Jade the way he had tried to throw me at the riding club, Jade could end up getting hurt.

After a few hours, I gave up on trying to sleep. I switched on my bedside lamp and picked up my newest horse magazine. Maybe if I read for a while, I would start to feel sleepy.

I flipped through the pages. I had read most of the articles already, but I never got tired of staring at photographs of magnificent horses and ponies.

The shots were a mix of horses of all shapes and sizes, from regal black stallions, rearing up with their legs waving in the air, to cute, shaggy ponies staring at the camera – right at me.

Towards the back of the magazine, my eyes fell on a shot of a young man wearing a cowboy hat. He sat on a golden palomino with an impossibly long flowing mane and a matching creamy white tail.

There was no saddle or bridle on the horse, just a thin rope looped around its neck, held high in one hand by the boy.

The horse stood proudly on a hilltop. Its ears were pricked, and its gaze was fixed on something in the distance. After a closer look, I realized it was an advertisement.

"Hike the Mountains on Horseback," it said.

The ad was for a guided trail ride in the mountains. It promised quiet, well-behaved horses and ponies for all levels of riding ability, as well as spectacular scenery, on a working cattle farm called Woodland Hills.

I read through the details before my gaze returned to the palomino. The horse was stunning.

In my mind, I removed the cowboy from the horse's back and put myself in his place. It would be so incredible to be sitting on that horse on that hilltop!

Then I took a deep breath. I had just had an idea.

At first I dismissed it. There was no chance. It could never happen.

But then again, why not? What if Jade and I went on a trail ride together? That would be a great way for Jade to learn to ride without using Bobby.

A weekend away with Jade would be fun, I mused. *And I could help Jade learn to ride as we go on the trails.*

The magazine slipped from my hand as sleep finally overtook me. That night, I dreamed of riding a beautiful palomino horse over a windswept hillside.

* * *

The next day, I couldn't stop thinking about the cowboy on the palomino. I wanted to go on that trip. It was the perfect idea.

I called Jade immediately after I finished eating breakfast. "How would you like to go on a horse-riding adventure?" I asked as soon as she picked up.

"What?" Jade asked. "Annie, what are you talking about? I thought you said I couldn't ride Bobby."

"You can't, but I have another idea. Listen to this." I read the advertisement to Jade. When I was finished, there was silence on the line.

"So," I said. "What do you think?"

"Hmmm," Jade said finally. "There's just one problem."

I was now so excited about the idea that I'd begun to mentally pack my bag while I was talking to Jade. I would need sun cream, and snacks for the trail, and of course I'd need to bring my riding helmet, and. . .

"Problem?" I repeated. "What problem? I can't think of a single one."

"Did you forget about our parents?" said Jade. "Do you think they'll let us go?"

I sighed. Jade was right.

It had just seemed like such a perfect solution. But I knew our parents could shut down the whole idea in an instant.

Still, I wasn't going to give up so easily. "What if they agreed?" I pressed. "Would you go?"

Jade snorted. "What do you think?" she asked sarcastically. "Of course I would."

"You start working on your parents, and give me a day or two to talk mine into it. I'll be in touch," I promised.

"Good luck," Jade said.

I knew she wasn't sure we could pull it off. And that just made me even more determined to try.

Next, it was time to tackle Mum and Dad.

I found my mum washing dishes in the kitchen. I picked up a tea towel and started helping.

"Hi, honey," Mum said. "How nice of you to help me."

"No problem, Mum!" I said.

"Are you excited for Jade to come next weekend?" she asked.

"Definitely," I told her. "That reminds me. I was thinking it would be really cool to go on a trail ride in the mountains with Jade while she's here."

"No, no, and no," my mum said.

"But, Mum," I whined. "You haven't heard anything about it yet."

"I've heard enough already," said my mother.

"You don't even have to drive us there," I said. "I found this place, and they meet their guests at the train station. Everything is totally supervised. We'll be completely safe."

"Annie, a trip like that is going to be very expensive. How were you planning on paying for it?" she asked.

I winced. That was something I hadn't thought about. The ad in the magazine hadn't said anything about the cost.

"I'll pay for it," I said. "With the money I earn from working at Erica's. And I know Jade will help. She gets an allowance. I'm sure between the two of us we can cover it."

My mum shook her head. She said, "Annie, I can't imagine this trail ride you're talking about would be cheap enough for Jade's allowance – or even your job at the stables – to cover."

"Mum, I work really hard at the stables," I said. "Ask Erica. She'll tell you. And I bet I could pick up some extra work with her after the holidays. I'll do whatever it takes. I really, really, really want to go."

My mum sighed. She was quiet for a while, washing another plate.

"Tell you what," she said finally. "If you can get your father to agree, we'll check it out."

I squealed. Mum quickly added, "But I'm not making any promises, so don't get your hopes up."

I basically ignored my mother's final sentence. As far as I was concerned, that was one parent down, one to go.

Chapter Four

I waited until we were halfway through dinner that night before bringing up the mountain trail ride.

I had expected my dad to argue with me about the idea of Jade and me travelling alone, but his main concern was a completely unexpected one.

The first thing he said was, "What about Bobby? Who'll look after him if you go on this trip?"

My mother and I stopped chewing our chicken and stared at my dad in amazement. I was shocked. My dad usually acted as if Bobby was a waste of space. He always complained that Bobby took away the grass in the paddock from his flock of six sheep. And now he was concerned about who would take care of Bobby?

"Rob," my mum said sharply. "Did you hear what Annie said? She wants to take Jade and go riding in the mountains with strangers."

That's when I realized that my mother had never intended to actually allow me to go on the trail ride. She'd been counting on my dad to say I couldn't go. I couldn't believe it! That was so mean.

"Oh, I don't know," my dad said thoughtfully. "These kinds of things are usually well supervised. It's a business, you know, Susan. The owners can't afford to have their customers getting into trouble."

I nodded. I was thrilled. I could tell that my father was actually thinking about it.

"So what's the name of this company, and how much is it all going to cost?" my father wanted to know.

"It's called Horse Hike Adventures," I said quickly. "It's at a farm called Woodland Hills. I'm not sure how much it is, but I'll put in all my pay from working at the stables if you'll let me go."

My father didn't say anything for a while as he moved the food around on his plate. "Well," he said finally, "I suppose I could make up the rest of the cost. But you still haven't answered me about Bobby."

I thought fast. "Reese," I said. "Reese will take care of him."

My father seemed happy with that. He puffed out his chest and spoke in his official estate agent voice. "All right then," he said. "How about you get me the telephone number, and I'll make some calls. If the place seems all right, I'll talk to Jade's parents about it."

"Are you sure, Rob?" my mum asked nervously. "Do you really think the girls are old enough to do this?"

"Well, yes, I do," Dad answered. "I think we try to wrap these kids in bubble wrap, Susan. Well, Annie's not the same kid she was when we first moved here. She's a responsible horse owner and has a part-time job now. I think we have to give her a chance."

Mum looked from Dad to me and then back again. "All right," she said slowly, then waved a finger at me. "But you have to take care of Jade. She has no riding experience at all."

"It's okay, Mum," I said. "We'll be careful. You won't have a thing to worry about."

I jumped up from my place at the table and hugged my father. "Thanks, Dad," I whispered. "You're the best!"

* * *

Before I knew it, it was Friday morning. I was going to pick up Jade at the Willowvale train station that afternoon.

My dad had called Woodland Hills and had a long talk with the manager. He asked them a tonne of questions. Where would we sleep? Who would supervise the riding? What safety precautions did they take?

Luckily, Dad had seemed satisfied with the answers. Then he'd called Jade's mum to tell her about it and discuss the hike. Unbelievably, she'd agreed that Jade could come.

The week had flown by with many phone calls between Jade and me about what we should pack. Finally, the day had arrived.

"Don't worry about a thing. I'll look after Bobby like he's my own horse," Reese promised as I unhooked the latch on Jefferson's gate.

Jefferson greeted Bobby with a low nicker. Reese opened the gate, pushing Jefferson back to allow me through with Bobby. My dog, Jonesy, stayed close to me. Once he would have chased the horses, but he'd learned the hard way – after a few well-aimed kicks – that the horses really didn't want to be friends with him.

I had brought Bobby over to stay at Reese's place while I was away. I wanted to make sure my horse was settled in before I left.

"Thank you so much for doing this," I said to Reese as I unbuckled Bobby's halter and slipped it off him.

Bobby and Jefferson arched their necks and sniffed each other's noses. Then the pair trotted off together to the far corner of the paddock.

"No problem," said Reese. She gave me a playful grin and added, "Bobby will enjoy his break even more with another horse for company. And you can go off on your boring old trail ride knowing he's in safe hands."

"I wish you could come, too," I said.

Reese shoved her hands into the pockets of her jacket and shook her head. "Three's a crowd," she told me. "Anyway, remember the last time we were all together?"

I nodded. I remembered all too well.

I had once spent a weekend with Reese and Jade. My two friends were as different as leather and lace. Reese thought Jade was a city snob, and Jade had thought Reese a country bore.

Reese felt around in her pocket and pulled out a chocolate bar. She pushed the chocolate into my pocket. "Take this," she said. "You might need an energy boost while you're away."

"Thanks," I said. I took one last look at Bobby, now happily grazing nose to nose with Jefferson. Then I waved goodbye to Reese and slipped through the fence to return home.

* * *

The train ride that afternoon was a rolling trip past miles of flat fields. The terrain got steeper and steeper as we travelled further into the mountains.

Outside the window, we saw that the train was going past herds of cows and huge fields of half-grown crops. We went through one small city, but after that, the houses started to get further and further apart.

Occasionally, the train would pass by huge orchards full of fruit trees. We also sped past a few big wineries with old brick mansions and rows of grapevines lining either side of the railroad tracks.

Jade and I had stocked up on snacks before catching the train, even though my mum had packed lunchboxes full of fruit and sandwiches for the trip.

We had plenty to catch up on and talked non-stop. I kept Jade amused with stories about riding club competitions, while Jade filled me in on everything that had been happening at my old school.

It seemed like hardly any time had passed, but suddenly, I felt the train slowing down. We were getting closer to our destination. A voice came over the PA system announcing that we were arriving at Woodland Hills.

"Are we here already?" asked Jade. "I thought the trip was two hours."

"It was," I said, checking my watch.

Jade peered out of the window. She shook her head, motioning for me to take a look. "This can't be right," she said. "The only thing out there is trees."

I looked outside at a dense forest of towering trees that lined both sides of the tracks. As the train slowed down, a platform appeared, then a rusty, bent sign, painted with the name "Woodland Hills." The train squealed to a stop.

Jade and I reached up to the luggage racks and pulled down our bags. A riding helmet hung from the strap of my bag. Even though the horse hike place had promised to supply helmets, I had wanted to bring my own.

We got off the train. After waiting for a minute, the train departed, leaving us staring after it. In eerie silence, we stood on a disturbingly empty platform.

"Well, here we are," I said.

"I thought someone was supposed to meet us," said Jade. She pulled her bags closer to her.

"So did I," I said. I checked my watch. Trying to stay positive, I said, "Well, I'm sure someone will be here soon."

I stared back down the tracks. I was pretty sure there wouldn't be another train for hours. Someone would turn up any minute. Right?

Somewhere in the trees, a bird called. I heard a rustling noise. Then, suddenly, a voice came from out of nowhere.

"You girls look like you need a ride," a boy's voice said.

Jade and I turned away from the platform to see a boy, not much older than us, slouched on the back of a palomino horse.

I recognized him instantly as the boy from the ad. I thought that the horse was even more beautiful than he had looked in the photo. Sitting at the feet of the horse was a grinning brown collie dog.

The boy wore jeans and a checked shirt. I noticed that he wasn't wearing a riding helmet. Instead, there was a wide-brimmed cowboy hat on his head.

Erica and the other instructors from Ridgeview would have been horrified. Nobody at my riding club would dream of getting on a horse without a helmet. It was the number-one safety requirement, and we all knew that.

"Where did you come from?" I asked.

The boy pointed to an uneven mud track that led through the trees. "That way," he said.

The sound of an engine broke through the stillness. The boy sat up taller in the saddle as a dusty old Jeep came rattling along the track. A short, round woman with curly red hair stepped out of the Jeep. She was dressed in jeans, too. Her shirt was blue cotton and looked like a man's work shirt. On her feet were sturdy boots.

"Welcome to Woodland Hills," the woman said. She walked up to Jade and me, reaching out her hand to take our bags.

"I'm Rita," she told us. "The brat on the horse is my son, Ben."

The woman turned to Ben. "I'll take the girls back in the Jeep," she said. "And how many times have I told you to wear your helmet when you're riding?"

"Sorry, Mum," said Ben, not sounding sorry at all.

Jade and I introduced ourselves. Then Ben lifted his reins in one hand and leaned a little to the left. Narrowly missing the dog with its hooves, the horse quickly turned on its haunches and disappeared down the trail in a slow lope.

There was a low whistle, and then the dog followed Ben.

"All right, girls," Rita said. "Get in the truck. I bet you'll want to relax tonight and get lots of rest. First thing tomorrow, you're headed off on your mountain adventure."

Rita picked up our bags and tossed them into the Jeep. I climbed into the front passenger seat. Jade shared the back seat with the bags.

The Jeep bounced along the path, leaving a thick trail of dust behind it. The forest closed in around us. Shafts of sunlight made dimples on the road as it streamed through the gaps in the tree canopy above us.

"How far is it to your property?" I called. I had to yell over the noise of the engine.

Rita laughed and yelled back, "You're already on it! We have thousands of acres here, and we're a long way from neighbours. Lucky for us, the train runs right through the middle of the place," she said.

"You mean you have your very own train station?" asked Jade.

"Yup," Rita told her.

Jade and I looked at each other in awe. One thing was bothering me, though. So far, all I had seen of the place was trees.

"Where are the mountains?" I asked now.

"Oh, don't worry," said Rita calmly. "You can't miss them."

The Jeep finally emerged from the trees. Spread out before us was a scene of rolling hills that seemed to rise in folds of green pasture. High above, in a dramatic backdrop, the misty peaks of a smoky-blue mountain range stood watch over the world.

It was breathtaking.

Both Jade and I let out gasps of wonder at the view.

Rita smiled. "There are the mountains," she said. She looked over at me and added, "That view is pretty great, isn't it? The people who live around these parts get to look out over it every morning." Rita laughed. "It's a tough job, but someone has to do it," she added, winking.

Not far out of the forest, Rita stopped the Jeep at a metal farm gate. With the truck's engine idling, Rita shot me a glance. I suddenly realized that she wanted me to get out and open the gate.

"Oh, sorry," I said and scrambled out of the vehicle.

The Jeep drove through. As I closed the gate before getting back into the truck, I looked out across the vast area of bright green grass ahead of me.

I wonder where the house is, I thought.

I had never seen such an enormous field. It seemed like the only living thing for miles around was grass.

We drove over several hills before there was any sign of another boundary fence. Three gates and three equally huge fields later, the Jeep rolled over yet another hill.

"There's our place," Rita said.

The house was a long, sprawling building with wide porches. A large barn and a few smaller buildings stood nearby. As Rita drove up yet another hill to the house, I could see no other signs of life.

"So how many guests will be riding tomorrow?" I asked Rita.

Rita drove the Jeep onto a slab of concrete next to the house. She turned off the engine and turned to Jade and me. "About half a dozen," she said. "You've chosen a quiet time to come. Our groups will be much bigger in a few weeks. There will be staff arriving next week to help out over the busy season. But for now, it's just me and Ben running things. You two were the only guests to arrive by train," she went on. "The others are driving up in the morning."

"Cool!" said Jade.

Rita laughed good-naturedly. "Annie's father tells me that you haven't ridden before, Jade," she said, helping us lift our bags out of the truck. "Ben will keep an eye on you and give you some riding tips. That way, Annie, you can relax and enjoy yourself."

"Oh, that's very nice of you, but it's all right," I said. "I can teach Jade to ride."

"Well, I'll let you and Ben figure that one out," said Rita. "But he does know the horses and the land around here. You'll find out once you get up into the mountains that the terrain can be quite challenging, even for riders who have some experience."

I stayed quiet. I didn't want to argue with Rita. Obviously, she didn't realize what an experienced rider she was talking to.

Rita led Jade and me into the house through the back porch. A couple of open doors showed glimpses of an old-fashioned kitchen and an equally ancient bathroom.

Rita pushed open a door. The bedroom was small. Two single beds, with a large window in between, took up most of the room.

"I'm afraid there's no wardrobe," Rita apologized. "But you'll be camping out in sleeping bags tomorrow night, so there's no point unpacking your bags. In the morning, just bring your sleeping things with you to breakfast – that'll be in the kitchen. You'll want to travel light on your ride."

I was startled by this news. My father hadn't said anything about camping out.

"Dinner will be served in the kitchen in about half an hour. You can use the bathroom to freshen up, if you need to," Rita said. She pointed back along the hall, in the direction we had just come from. Then she left.

Jade ran her hand over one of the beds. Instead of comfortable duvets, each bed was covered with faded old bedspreads. Jade pushed at the mattress. It let out a loud squeak.

The light from outside was beginning to fade as darkness fell. I found a switch by the door and flicked on the light.

As soon as Rita was out of the room, Jade turned to me, a huge frown on her face. "Nobody told me we'd be sleeping outside in sleeping bags," she said. "I hate camping."

"Sorry, didn't I tell you?" I said quickly. I didn't want to admit that I hadn't known either. "I guess it would take too long to ride up to the mountains and back again in one day."

"But what about bugs? And spiders?" Jade asked. She shivered. "What about snakes?" she whispered.

I shivered, too, imagining a snake slithering into my sleeping bag. "It can't be that bad," I said. "If that boy Ben can do it, then I'm sure we can, too."

At the mention of Ben's name, Jade giggled.

"What?" I asked.

"Oh, nothing," said Jade. She looked around, and then whispered, "It's just . . . didn't you think Ben was kind of . . . cute?"

I punched Jade sharply on the arm and told her, "If you want to learn to ride, you'd better concentrate on the horses."

* * *

That night, Rita served us a delicious meal of baked pasta, followed by ice cream with chocolate sauce.

The three of us ate at an old, rectangular wooden table in the kitchen. There was no sign of Ben.

"Ben will eat later," Rita explained. "He's in the tack room, getting the gear ready for tomorrow's ride."

After brushing our teeth and changing into pyjamas, Jade and I climbed into our beds.

"Is your bed lumpy?" Jade complained. "Seriously, this is not what I expected. I've never had a holiday like this before!"

"I didn't say we were staying at the Hilton," I answered with a yawn. I felt myself drifting into sleep. "Is it really that bad?" I mumbled.

But if Jade replied, I wasn't awake to hear it.

* * *

Jade and I woke early. I dressed in my riding outfit – jodhpurs, a long-sleeved T-shirt, and the riding vest that I'd worn the day before. Jade had borrowed an old pair of my jodhpurs and paired them with a T-shirt and a polar fleece jacket. The jodhpurs had once belonged to Reese, but I didn't tell Jade that.

I slipped my hands into the pocket of my vest and felt the chocolate bar that Reese had given me. For a moment, I felt really sad that my friend from Ridgeview wasn't here. Reese would have loved this whole scene.

Rita had told us to bring our clothes to breakfast, so Jade and I grabbed the things we would need for an overnight trip. We left the rest of our things in the room and headed for the kitchen.

After a breakfast of scrambled eggs and hash browns, Rita gave us each a plastic bag for our things and directed us to the big barn we had seen the day before.

Inside, the barn was a well-organized stable block. There were separate areas for washing horses and storing feed and hay. There was also a whole wall where dozens of saddles, bridles, and various other pieces of tack hung from hooks.

Ben was nowhere to be seen. Six horses – already saddled, bridled and tied to a rail – stood patiently waiting outside the stables.

"Oh, cool," said Jade when she saw the horses. "I wonder which one's mine?"

My gaze was more critical. The horses, all blacks and bays except for one grey, had been roughly groomed. A couple of them still had twigs and bits of dried grass caught in their tails. They looked quiet enough, but none had the grace and presence of the palomino that Ben rode. I sensed, though, that these horses would be perfectly suited to Jade's riding ability.

I no longer thought of myself as a beginner. I wanted to ride a horse with spirit. I cast my eyes over the saddles worn by the horses. Each saddle had a neatly rolled sleeping bag strapped behind it. Though they looked clean, all the saddles were shabby and worn.

They're even worse than my old saddle, I thought.

I had been forced to purchase secondhand gear when I'd first started riding. It was my dream to one day save enough money to buy a brand new, top-of-the-range saddle.

The dog came out from one of the stables. It greeted us with a wagging tail and a sharp bark.

"Hello, boy," I said. Seeing the little dog made me miss Jonesy. I patted my thighs in an invitation for the dog to jump up.

"Don't do that," a boy's voice said.

I looked around in surprise. Ben appeared at the door of one of the horse stalls.

A golden head popped up behind him. I drew in my breath sharply. The palomino. I stared over Ben's shoulder at the horse.

"Please don't play with my dog," Ben said. "That's a working dog, not a pet."

Surprised, I stepped back, away from the dog. "Oh, I'm really sorry! I was just being friendly," I said.

"Hey," Jade said, smiling at Ben. "Cool dog. What's his name?"

Ben turned to Jade. "Thanks," he said. "He's a she. Her name's Jack."

"Jack!" I blurted out. "What sort of a name is that for a female dog?"

"It's her name. I like it," Ben said. He glared at me.

"I think I'll call her Jackie," I said.

"If you leave her alone, you can call her whatever you want." Ben's words held a warning undertone that I couldn't fail to notice.

Ben was horrible, I decided. Even if Jade did think he was cute.

A car pulled up outside the barn. We heard the sound of four doors closing, and then voices. At the same moment, there was a snort from the palomino. Ben turned back and gently caressed his horse's muzzle.

"Midas, it sounds like the rest of our guests have arrived," said Ben.

So that's his name, I thought. Midas suited the golden horse. It was a much better name than Ben had given the poor dog.

Four people, all much older than Jade and me, walked into the barn. I noticed right away that Ben's attitude changed quickly from grumpy to welcoming as he greeted the newest guests to arrive.

The first members of the group were a man and a woman wearing jeans, western-style shirts, and cowboy hats like the one Ben had been wearing the day before. Ben introduced them as Rachel and William.

The pair seemed very familiar with Ben. They mentioned that they had been to the farm a couple of times. This time they had brought along some friends – another couple.

The second man was tall and wore glasses. He wore a pair of cream-coloured pants and expensive-looking boots. He kept breaking into nervous laughter.

"I'm Sam, hehehe. This is my wife, Joanne, hehehe. I have to warn you, Ben," the man said, "we're both beginners. We don't have a clue about how to ride a horse, but we've always thought it would be a good way to see some countryside." Then Sam added, "Can't be that hard to learn, though. Hehehe."

Sam's wife was wearing jodhpurs, just like Jade and me. I was the only one who had brought along my own riding helmet.

Ben handed out helmets for the other people to try on. "You'll need to wear these at all times when you're on your horses," he said.

While they were all checking the helmets for fit, Ben kept talking. "We need to match you guys up with horses according to your experience. Then we can get this ride moving. How many of you are beginners?" he asked.

Sam, Joanne, and Jade raised their hands. "All right," Ben said. "Why don't all of you head outside to wait? I'll get your horses ready."

As we walked out of the barn, I looked up at the sky. The day was warming up fast. Brilliant sunshine shone down on the farm. I was struck once again by the amazing view. *It must be so incredible to live in a place like this,* I thought.

One by one, Ben led the horses out of the barn and into a large yard. Then Ben helped each rider to mount and sent them off to practice walking around in circles.

The horses hardly needed any direction, I noticed. They looked as if they'd done this a thousand times before, which they probably had. It was their job, after all.

I watched Rachel and William. They sat on their horses easily and appeared quietly confident. Sam and Joanne looked nervous, but their horses seemed calm enough.

Next, Ben helped Jade up onto a tall, black horse.

"His name is Oscar," Ben told Jade. "He's really quiet, and I promise he'll take good care of you. All you have to do is sit back and enjoy the ride."

"Okay," Jade said quietly. I noticed that she was staring intently into Ben's eyes.

I think I might be sick, I thought meanly.

This weekend trail ride was supposed to be a chance for Jade and me to catch up. But now, I was beginning to worry that Jade might conveniently forget all about me since Ben was around.

Not fair, I thought. *This is supposed to be a trip for two friends, not a matchmaking service for Jade.* I wished again that Reese had come along.

Jade was white-faced as she stared down at Oscar's neck. The horse moved forward after the others, while Jade leaned forward and clung to his mane.

I'll have to show Jade how to sit the right way, I thought.

I was the only person left without a horse. "Okay, Annie, I'll be right back," Ben said.

"Okay," I said.

Ben disappeared into the barn. I couldn't wait to see him lead the golden horse, Midas, out and let me ride him.

When Ben returned with the grey horse, I almost gasped with disappointment. The horse was obviously really old. Even though it was almost summertime, long, leftover chunks of winter coat still hung off the horse in places. It didn't look anything like that golden glory, Midas.

I glanced over at Jade's black horse with dismay. Compared to this bedraggled horse in front of me, Jade's horse suddenly looked much more appealing.

"Don't let looks fool you," said Ben. "Old Bandit here is the best of the bunch. I'm only letting you to ride him because you told us you were experienced."

"Gee, thanks," I said with a bitter smile.

I decided that my "great idea" of taking Jade for a horse hike in the mountains had been a completely stupid one. First of all, I had been given the plainest, oldest, and probably most useless horse, and I'd be stuck with it for the next two days. Plus, Jade wasn't even interested in hanging out with me, now that she'd decided that Ben was so cute.

I thought about Ben riding his gorgeous Midas. That was the horse I should be riding this weekend.

My mood didn't improve once I was on Bandit's back. I wiggled in the saddle, trying to force the hard leather of the stock saddle to soften. The reins felt rough and worn.

Adding to my sense of discomfort were the saddlebags that hung behind my legs from each side of the saddle flaps.

I suddenly felt a new appreciation for my own secondhand dressage saddle. I still hated it, but at least it was more comfortable to sit in than this!

Thank goodness I brought my own helmet, I thought.

Ben began walking from rider to rider. With each rider, he made sure that the girth was tight on the saddles. He handed out packs, explaining how to tie them to the front of each saddle.

Ben handed me one of the packs. It was rolled up and secured tightly with brown twine. There was a piece of fabric shoved inside.

"What's this?" I asked.

"Your heavy riding coat," said Ben. "You'll be glad you have it, trust me."

I looked pointedly up at the sky. It was already pretty warm out.

"A coat?" I repeated. "By the look of things, we'll all be taking off our sweaters by lunchtime. By the way, Jade and I left our stuff in the barn," I added, thinking of my pajamas and toothbrush. I didn't want to leave them behind.

"I stuffed your pajamas and stuff inside your sleeping bags," said Ben. "And don't be fooled by the weather. You're in mountain country now. The weather can change in an instant."

Ben disappeared into the barn. A moment later, he returned, mounted on Midas. I stared jealously at the horse's rich golden coat and fluid white mane and tail.

"Let's get going," Ben called out. "My mum will be driving up to meet us later at the campsite. She'll bring all your bags with her in the Jeep."

Ben mounted up and took the lead, ordering everyone to follow at a walk. Even though the morning had started badly, I shivered with excitement. We were finally on our way.

The beginners, Jade included, were looking around nervously at each other. I grinned, feeling proud. I felt like I knew exactly what I was doing.

Ben led the group out across an open field behind the house. Jack ran on ahead, stopping from time to time to sniff or dig.

"Stay behind me," Ben commanded everyone. "Once we get going, we can pick up the pace a little bit."

Jade had steered her horse into position next to Ben and Midas. Oscar plodded steadily over the grass. I could see how gentle and quiet he was. His perfect manners would be good for Jade. I could see that Jade was already beginning to relax.

"I think I'm going to enjoy today," Jade said to Ben, who nodded.

"I hope you do," he said, smiling.

The older couples were speaking softly among themselves. Once in a while, I'd hear Sam's anxious laugh.

Bandit walked along quietly, lagging behind Oscar and Midas.

I didn't want to be left out of the conversation, so I used my legs to squeeze Bandit's sides and trot up to the other side of Jade.

"I thought I told you to walk," said Ben, looking over at me and frowning.

"I was just catching up," I retorted. "I wanted to ride next to my friend," I added, looking pointedly at Jade.

"Well, please remember that the other horses might want to follow you," said Ben briskly. "I don't want anybody falling off."

"Does that happen often?" Jade asked nervously.

"Not often. I try to look after our guests, and we have good, quiet horses," said Ben, patting Midas's head. "But it only takes one idiot to wreck everything."

I felt my face getting hot. Now Ben was calling me an idiot. How dare he!

I decided to ignore him, so I turned my attention to Jade. Now that we were on our way, it was a good time to give Jade some riding advice. After all, that's why we'd come on this trip.

"Now, Jade," I began, "while your horse is walking along, push your heels down. Sit up really tall and put your shoulders back."

Instead of taking my advice, Jade looked to Ben. "Is that right, Ben?" Jade asked.

My eyes widened in anger. Before Ben could respond, I quickly cut in. "Jade, I thought you wanted me to teach you to ride," I said. "I mean, that's why I organized this trip."

Jade shook her head. "I did, but I wanted you to teach me how to ride Bobby," she explained. "But this isn't Bobby. This is Ben's horse. And we're not in Ridgeview. It's probably better if Ben shows me how to ride his horse in the mountains. Don't you think? I mean, that's what Rita was saying yesterday."

"It doesn't really matter who the horses belong to," I said, my voice rising a little. "Riding is riding, after all."

Ben frowned. "That's not really true," he said calmly.

I rolled my eyes and frowned. "Oh, really," I snapped.

"You belong to a riding club, don't you?" asked Ben.

I nodded impatiently. I didn't see what that had to do with anything.

Ben continued. "I ride out here in the open spaces. Sometimes I'm on the farm, working with cattle. When we have guests I take them up into the mountains," he said.

"What does that have to do with anything?" I asked, looking away angrily.

Ben dropped his reins onto Midas's neck. He looked pointedly at my hands. I didn't know my horse yet. I didn't know he'd behave. So I was holding Bandit's reins firmly.

"When I teach a guest how to ride," Ben continued, watching my hands, "the first thing I like to teach them is to relax."

Instantly, my grip on Bandit's reins loosened. On her horse, Jade was staring from Ben to me, watching us.

"So you think I should hold my reins loose like yours, Ben?" Jade asked now.

"I think it's what your horse would like," Ben said. "He knows where he has to go, and he'll be a whole lot more comfortable if you're not pulling him in the mouth. Up here in the mountains, there's not much need for all that fancy kind of riding."

"I wasn't pulling him in the mouth, and my riding isn't fancy!" I fired back at Ben. "I ride the way I've been taught by a very experienced dressage instructor who says I should keep contact at all times."

We had walked across the field and come to a gate. Ben ignored my last comment and leaned over Midas's neck to open the gate.

He pushed it back to allow everyone to ride through, then skilfully steered his horse into position so he could close the gate again.

Then Ben spoke to the group. "Is everyone ready to try to trot?" he asked.

The others nodded. I didn't bother responding. Of course I was ready to trot. I was ready for any kind of riding.

Ben pointed to the left of the new field we were now standing in. The ground sloped upwards in a gentle rise.

"All right then," said Ben. "Let's go."

Midas stayed ahead of the other horses. If any horse attempted to pass him, he would lay his ears flat against his head, warning them to stay back.

Jade giggled nervously when Oscar broke into a trot. She was bouncing all over the saddle but miraculously staying balanced enough to not fall out of it.

"Just let all your weight fall into your legs," Ben told us.

Watching, I wanted to shout at Ben. That wasn't the way I had been taught. What about rising up and down to the two-time beat of the trot?

As our group trotted over the next rise, the open fields came to an end, and the mountains were suddenly towering over us. The trees became more plentiful, and the pasture thinned as we headed towards yet another gate.

"Whoa!" Ben called out when he reached the gate. Once again, he opened the gate from Midas's back. Then he turned to face the rest of us.

"This is the eastern boundary of Woodland Hills," Ben explained to his guests. "From now on, we'll be climbing up the side of Mount Tantara. We should reach the moors by mid-afternoon, but we'll stop for lunch at about one."

Ben directed the riders into a single file. He put Jade and Oscar behind himself and Midas. Following Jade was Sam, then Joanne, Rachel, and William. I was last in line, behind William.

I urged Bandit towards Jade. I was about to squeeze him in between Jade and Sam when Ben stopped me.

"Annie, I'd like you to stay last in line. I need someone with experience back there, just in case."

I felt like arguing. I wanted to be near my friend. It annoyed me that Ben thought he could just order me around. I was the customer, so why should I be taking orders from Ben?

But I couldn't think of a way I could object without sounding completely lame. I slowed Bandit and waited for the others to pass me before joining back up at the end of the line.

As soon as we passed the Woodland Hills
boundary, the land changed dramatically. In
single file, along a dark and narrow trail, the
steadily climbing group passed through a heavily
wooded forest.

I felt left out. I could hear Jade and Ben up
ahead, talking and laughing. The older couples,
Rachel and William and Sam and Joanne,
chatted among themselves.

For a while, I listened in. At first they
discussed their horse-riding experiences. Rachel

was telling Joanne how fantastic the views were up on the moors.

I noticed with annoyance that the men, especially Sam, didn't seem to care much about the horses. Sam kept making dumb jokes as if the horses were cars.

"Hehehe, I think this horse needs an oil change," he'd say, or "I wonder when the brakes were last checked on this thing? Hehehe." It was so annoying.

I patted Bandit's pale neck, as if I were apologizing for the stupidity of Sam's remarks. Even though I had been disappointed to be riding Bandit, I still thought all horses deserved to be treated with respect.

When the couples started talking about the stock market, I tuned out. That was way too boring. Instead, I tried to pay more attention to my surroundings.

The trail was always changing. It twisted and turned, winding its way ever upwards past thick pockets of undergrowth and sudden grassy clearings, where the sun would light up a patch of grass like a spotlight.

Often, fallen logs crossed our path. Some of the logs were quite big, but the horses didn't seem to notice. They just lifted their feet a little higher and stepped over them as if the big logs were twigs.

I began to admire the horses. Even though Sam was leaning too far to one side and Joanne was constantly grabbing at her horse's mouth by pulling on the reins, the horses all plodded on regardless, one after another.

I guessed that the horses must have carried dozens of inexperienced riders along these trails. They knew their job well.

That made me think about Bobby. He'd been so patient, back when I started riding. Although

I hoped Bobby was enjoying his rest, I couldn't help but wish I were riding him now, instead of Bandit.

"We'll trot again up here," Ben yelled back from the front. "Stop when you come to the river crossing. We'll eat lunch there."

The horses were well-trained. They all trotted in line.

I'd had enough. I'd come on this ride to spend time with Jade, but Jade's attention seemed focused on Ben. I heard her giggling up ahead at something Ben was saying.

That just made me feel angrier. It was like she didn't even care that we weren't spending our trip together.

I heard the river crossing before I saw it. The sound of water falling over rocks and rushing downstream made everyone exclaim with delight.

Even though I'd worked myself into a bad mood, I couldn't help admiring the beauty of the running stream as the sparkling clear water made its way down to lower countryside.

The riders stopped at a clearing beside the river. Huge boulders were scattered along the river bank.

We all dismounted. I led Bandit to the river, where he drank briefly. The others followed my lead.

After the horses finished drinking, the other riders found long pieces of baling twine already tied to some of the trees. Using the reins, they tied their horses to the twine.

I did the same, but I wasn't too happy about it. It just made me nervous. It didn't seem secure enough. Erica had taught me to always use a halter and lead rope in case the horse pulled back and broke the reins.

Ben instructed everyone to loosen the horses' girths and look inside our saddlebags. "You'll find lunch in there," he said.

I reached inside my saddlebag and pulled out a smaller bag made of canvas. Inside were some hay cubes.

When I held the bag up, I realized with satisfaction that it was actually a nosebag for Bandit. I felt a little bit better knowing the horses had lunch to eat.

Ben had taken Jack and walked off into the forest. Jade was tying up Oscar. I found a couple of sandwiches inside my other saddlebag. Taking them with me, I went to see Jade.

"Hey! How's it going in the back?" Jade asked.

I shrugged. "It's okay," I said.

"Is this tied up the right way?" Jade asked, pointing to the knot in Oscar's reins.

"Why don't you ask Ben?" I blurted out angrily.

Jade looked puzzled for a moment, then said uncertainly, "Okay. I will."

Ben appeared. "Ask me what?" he said.

Jade showed Ben her knot. Ben studied the knot. Then he untied it and showed Jade how to tie it so that the horse couldn't pull back and get away.

"Oscar won't go anywhere," he said as he finished tying the new knot. "He's a good horse. But you might as well learn how to do it the right way."

I rolled my eyes. When it came to horses, plenty of Ben's "right" ways were a lot different to the way I'd been taught.

I had hoped to eat my lunch with Jade. But when Ben found a large, flat boulder to sit on, Jade sat down beside him. I walked off.

"Hey," Jade called to me. "Where are you going?"

"Oh, just checking on my horse," I mumbled. Increasing my speed, I moved away from Ben, Jade, and the others. I returned to where Bandit stood, quietly munching from his nosebag. I stuffed the sandwich back inside my saddlebag. Then I sat down, using the opposite side of Bandit's tree as a backrest.

I closed my eyes. I figured if I pretended I was having a nap, then everyone, including Jade, would leave me alone. But when they did, I just felt disappointed.

After lunch, the group of beginners seemed more confident. Ben picked up the pace, letting everyone trot where the trail wasn't too rough.

"When can we see what these babies can really do? Hehehehe," Sam called out to Ben as we trotted along in single file.

"We can let the horses stretch their legs once we're up on the moors," Ben called back.

Sam and the others nodded. Everyone seemed happy for Ben to control the speed of the ride. Everyone except me. The way I saw it, Jade had deserted me for Ben, and I'd been stuck being a babysitter for a bunch of boring adults. This wasn't the trip I'd planned.

The trail dipped down into a steep gully and then rose sharply upwards again. Ben told us all to slow to a walk.

The trees thinned out and the sun was suddenly hot on my neck. I brought Bandit to a halt so I could take off my vest. I stuffed the vest into a saddlebag.

The others disappeared around the next bend. No one noticed when I stopped.

Bandit wanted to catch up with his friends, but I stopped him. Off to the right, the trail split and formed a fork. It stretched away and then bent back on itself to the left. I peered as far as I could down the new trail. *It's probably just a detour,* I thought.

The trail to my right was smooth and sandy. It looked a lot better than the rough stones I was on.

I bit my lip, thinking. It was a chance to experience some freedom, maybe get some time to canter. Ben wouldn't be there to boss me around. I could get a break from everyone, and I could latch back on to the end of the group further up.

I made a decision. Using my right rein to turn Bandit, I steered him towards the new path. Bandit was reluctant. He kept looking in the direction the other riders had gone.

"Come on, Bandit. It's just for a little while. You'll be back with all your friends before you know it," I told the horse.

I had to pull hard on the reins to make him go, but eventually Bandit gave up and allowed himself to be taken in the new direction.

Great, I thought to myself rebelliously. *Now, I can finally have some fun.*

Chapter Ten

I urged Bandit into a canter. The horse obeyed, but he didn't seem very excited about it.

He probably isn't used to being asked to ride alone, I thought. *He's used to riding with the pack, with the rest of his friends.*

The thought made me feel sad. I wished I were riding with my friends from Ridgeview. I wondered what Reese was doing. Maybe she was out riding Jefferson now. And poor Bobby was all alone.

Bandit's hooves struck the ground with rhythmic thuds. As we moved farther down the trail, the horse gradually loosened up and seemed happier to go.

He began to canter faster. I didn't try to slow him down.

I was enjoying the freedom of riding alone, in a new location. I leaned over Bandit's neck and quickly pushed him into a gallop. Bandit responded eagerly. I could tell he really loved running.

We rounded a bend, but as soon as we did, I spotted yet another fallen log across the trail. This one was too big to step over, and we were going too fast to stop.

I asked Bandit to slow down a little. Then I clasped my legs tight to the horse's sides and looked ahead to a place on the other side of the fallen log.

"Let's see what you can do," I said to the horse as we raced towards the log.

The fallen tree loomed closer. I squeezed my legs on Bandit's sides and lifted myself out of the saddle so that I was leaning over his neck. Bandit launched and became airborne.

Suddenly, we were over the log and cantering on down the trail.

"Whoa!" I called to Bandit, slowly bringing him back to a trot, then a walk.

Bandit was breathing really hard from the run. Dark patches of sweat stained his neck and shoulders.

A rush of adrenaline surged through my body. That log had been bigger than anything I had ever jumped with Bobby.

I asked Bandit to halt and turned back to look at the log. I was pretty sure that it was as big as a B-rating cross-country jump. That was two levels higher than D-rating, the level I usually competed at.

Too bad Reese wasn't here to see that, I thought, pleased with myself.

Bandit gradually stopped puffing, and I became aware of the stillness. I had been so caught up with the excitement of my gallop that I had forgotten all about the rest of the group.

Now, in the sudden quiet, it occurred to me that I probably should have met up with the others by now.

I shivered as goosebumps broke out on my arms. It had grown colder. I reached into the saddlebag, pulled out my crumpled vest, and slipped it back on.

I tried to think logically about which direction I had travelled since leaving the group. The trail had twisted and turned so often. I really wasn't sure where I was or which way I'd gone.

example 95 example

I'll just follow the trail back, I thought. *The others are probably looking for me right now, so I can meet back up with them at the place I turned off.*

I turned Bandit and walked him back along the trail. This time I walked the horse carefully around the fallen log. I was still feeling good about the ease with which Bandit had cleared it. I couldn't wait to tell my friends back at the riding club!

There was a forking trail, leading off to the right. But then a few yards ahead, another trail forked away from the main path.

I frowned. I didn't remember seeing that trail before.

There were dozens of trails. I could have come down any one of them, but I had no way of knowing which one would lead me back to the others. I'd been concentrating on getting Bandit going faster and faster, instead of watching out for where I was going.

The sky was dark with clouds. I felt a drop of moisture land on my cheek, then another. It was starting to rain. The weather that had been so sunny and warm only a few hours earlier had turned.

I dismounted in a small clearing. My damp fingers fumbled with the knot in the baling twine as I worked to untie the bundle on the front of my saddle.

Ben was right about the weather, I thought.

Feeling embarrassed, I remembered how cranky I'd been about the heavy riding coat. I quickly unrolled the coat and slipped it on.

I wondered what to do next. The rain had made the unfamiliar territory look even more foreign.

I looked up through the tree canopy to the dull, cloudy sky. It looked like there were only a couple of daylight hours left.

Should I keep going, or stay put until the others find me? I wondered.

At the edge of the clearing, I spotted a large block of granite with a slight overhang. There was a dry patch of ground beneath the overhang. I decided to hide under the rock until the rain stopped.

Leading Bandit, I scrambled under the rock and sat down. Bandit stood outside the overhang.

Now that I was sitting, my hold on the reins was forcing the horse to dip his head low. He didn't look at all comfortable.

I looked around, wondering what to do with Bandit. My eyes rested on a cluster of trees.

That gave me an idea.

Dragging Bandit with me, I scrambled up and headed back out into the rain. I grabbed the twine that had been wrapped around the heavy riding coat.

Stringing the twine from tree to tree, I managed to build a small area for Bandit.

I led Bandit in and removed all his tack. Then I tied the reins from Bandit's bridle across the remaining gap in my homemade yard to act as a gate.

Bandit immediately began to graze around the yard, snatching at green grass growing around the base of the trees.

"Sorry I don't have more food for you," I told the horse.

I felt a twinge in my stomach. Talking about food was making me hungry, too.

I picked up the heavy saddle with the sleeping bag attached and carried it back to the rock. Once I was back under cover, I wiped a strand of wet hair away from my eyes. Then I dug back into the saddlebag to retrieve my uneaten sandwich from the lunch break.

I stared out from my little shelter. Large droplets of water fell in a tiny stream from the top of the rock. All around me was a constant dripping as the rain landed on leaves, then rolled off again into the undergrowth.

I finished my sandwich and lay back against the saddle. I stared out at the wet forest surrounding me. I banged at the ground with my fist. Stupid. I was stupid.

I'd only been thinking about myself. And why had I been so determined to show off?

I knew the answer, and was suddenly ashamed of myself.

I had wanted to show Jade just how far I'd come along as a rider, but there was something else. The truth was, I had been jealous of the way Jade and Ben were getting along.

Jealously had caused problems for me in the past. Sitting there in the rain, I made a promise to myself. I would try to never again make stupid decisions because of jealousy.

I was lost, and I really had no one else to blame but myself. Why had I thought I could go off on my own, in unfamiliar territory on a horse I hardly knew?

Pride and jealousy. Not a good combination.

The rain came down heavier. It would be dark soon. I curled up into a ball and huddled into the coat, trying to keep myself warm.

"Please, Jade. Please, Ben," I whispered. "Please come and find me soon."

Chapter Eleven

I woke to darkness and a loud snort nearby. It sounded like it came from the direction of Bandit's yard. The rain had stopped and strips of moonlight brightened the clearing.

I could see Bandit's shadow in the yard. He held his head high, and his eyes were fixed on something moving in the trees.

Whatever was in the trees suddenly moved away. I heard a crackle of undergrowth that retreated into the distance. Then everything was quiet and still once more.

Stiff and cold, I crawled out from under the rock ledge and stumbled over to Bandit's area. The horse, nostrils flaring, glanced briefly at me before returning his gaze to the bushes.

I stared in the same direction. I shuddered, wondering what kind of wild animal had been stalking me and Bandit while I'd slept.

With his tail arched and his tense body quivering, Bandit trotted the two strides across the yard to where I stood.

"Hey, Bandit. Whatever it was, it's gone now," I reassured the horse.

I stroked his nose and wondered what I should do now. I swallowed, my mouth uncomfortably dry from thirst.

"Poor horse," I whispered, moving my hand up to Bandit's ears and offering him a scratch. "You're thirsty, too, I bet. I'm so sorry. As soon as it's daylight we'll try and find water."

I shivered. Even though it was almost summer, the night was freezing on the mountain. I left the horse and returned to the rock. It was only then that I remembered the sleeping bag.

The moonlight cast strange shadows as I unrolled the sleeping bag. I took off the heavy coat and laid it out on top of the sleeping bag.

It was much warmer inside the sleeping bag, and lying on the thin mattress was way more comfortable than the bare ground. As I lay there, I tried not to let myself get spooked.

Daylight has to come soon, I thought. Ben and the others would have called for help by now. Maybe they'd sent out a search party.

I thought about Jade, probably asleep somewhere on the mountain with Ben and the others.

Then again, maybe the ride had been called off because I was missing.

Tears slid down my face. I hadn't even made it to the top of the mountain. And so much for bringing Jade on a horseback adventure! My friend was probably furious with me for ruining the trip.

I should have listened to Ben. I didn't even want to think about what he might say when I was found.

And then there were my parents. After this, they probably wouldn't let me go anywhere ever again.

I tried to imagine being tucked into my old bed – the one in the city. The streetlights would glow behind my curtains. Cars would still be rushing around during the night.

It seemed so far away and so long ago now. Suddenly the situation I was in didn't seem so scary. Even now, lost and alone, I preferred the peace and beauty of the forest to the noise and bustle of that other life.

When I woke up, it was morning.

Bandit greeted me with an anxious whinny as I emerged from under the rock ledge. I was still cold, and it was hard to make my fingers work to tighten the girth on Bandit's saddle and refasten the reins to his bridle.

The horse made my work even more difficult by nuzzling at me, looking for food. He'd cleaned up every blade of grass from the yard and was expecting breakfast.

"Sorry, buddy," I said. "I don't have any food for you. Or for me."

I rolled up the sleeping bag and tied it back on the saddle.

Fog had settled in the clearing while I slept. Grey streamers of mist hung among the tree branches. The air was chilly. I shrugged my arms back into the heavy riding coat.

Before leaving the clearing, I carefully collected all the baling twine from Bandit's yard. As I stuffed the twine back inside a saddlebag, I touched something that made a quiet crinkling sound.

I smiled. Reese's chocolate bar!

I pulled out the bar and was about to unwrap it when I stopped. I had no way of knowing how much longer I would be lost on this mountain. Maybe I should save it.

Sadly, I put the chocolate back in the saddlebag. I could make it a little while longer without food.

"Let's just get out of here, okay, boy?" I said. My words came out as a hoarse croak.

I put my foot into the stirrup and mounted. "But first," I added, "we'll look for water. I think we'll both feel better after we get something to drink."

I was still confused by all of the trails, which seemed to run all over the mountain. I reined Bandit to a halt and was wondering which direction to take when he suddenly made the decision for me.

He made a very definite turn, without any direction from me, and began walking purposefully down one particular trail.

I was about to stop him, but then I thought better of it. Maybe it would be a good idea to let him go and see where we ended up.

I'd read often enough that horses had incredible memories and a great sense of direction. I also knew from first-hand experience that it was true.

Bobby always seemed to know the way we were going whenever I rode him. Once we turned for home, his pace would pick up. He'd walk with more eagerness and excitement than he did when we were heading away from home.

Maybe I should just let Bandit decide where to take us, I thought. *After all, I have no idea where we are or where to go.*

I let the reins fall onto Bandit's neck and allowed him to take me where he wanted to go. We hadn't gone too far when I heard the welcome sound of running water.

Another river crossing!

"Hey," I yelled with delight as I realized what this meant.

Not only would we finally be able to drink, but if Bandit had found his way to water, maybe he'd take me all the way home.

"Good boy, Bandit!" I said happily. "You're the best!"

Bandit marched towards the water. I reached down and wrapped my arms around his strong neck.

"You're a smart horse," I told him. It occurred to me that Ben had been right all along about this horse.

Bandit had his head down and was drinking even before I could dismount. I followed his example. I got off and crouched down at the bank so I could slurp the water up through my hands.

All along the river bank, lush grass grew in thick clumps. Once Bandit had quenched his thirst with a good long drink, he strained at the reins, trying to reach the grass.

"You must be starving, huh, Bandit?" I said. "I know I am."

I allowed Bandit to tow me along the river bank so he could graze. My own stomach rumbled and I took the chocolate bar from the saddlebag. Like Bandit, I really needed to eat something.

Sending a silent thank you to Reese, I scoffed the chocolate and licked the remains from my fingers. It wasn't nearly enough to satisfy my growling stomach, but at least it was something. Now I could go on a little longer.

I looked at my watch. It was now late morning.

"Come on, Bandit," I said. I tugged his head up and away from the grass. "Time for you to show me the way back down this mountain."

I had my leg half over Bandit's back when something suddenly moved on the opposite river bank. Startled by the rustling noise, Bandit leaped sideways.

My foot slipped from the stirrup and I was thrown forward onto Bandit's neck. I felt my body slipping. Instinctively, I threw my arms around the horse's neck and clung on with my legs, saving myself from falling.

I pulled myself up and sat back into the saddle. Tense now, Bandit stared at the opposite bank.

Something was hiding in the grass, right on the edge of the bank near the track. My throat tightened nervously. I didn't know what kinds of animals lived out here, and I didn't really feel like finding out.

I had planned to ride Bandit across the shallow river and keep following the trail. I hoped that it would lead me back to Woodland Hills. But with something rustling across the river, I wasn't sure I wanted to go over there.

I had a couple of other options.

One was to stay where I was and hope that somebody found me.

My other choice was to go back to where I had camped at the rock overhang the night before.

None of them seemed like good ideas.

The grass rustled again. Whatever it was, it was small enough to not be seen. I decided it was probably a snake.

My stomach rumbled again and made the decision for me. I was too hungry to stay where I was. I had to move.

Chapter Twelve

Cautiously, Bandit and I entered the water. I kept my gaze on the grass, hoping that we could just ride quietly by and leave the snake undisturbed.

Bandit and I were halfway across the river when the thing in the grass moved again. I brought Bandit to a halt.

The slow-moving water swirled around the horse's legs. A grinning brown head popped up from the tuft of grass.

I had been holding my breath, and I let it all out in a giant-sized sigh of relief.

"Jackie!" I called out, laughing.

The dog jumped up from where she'd been crouching in the grass and bounced through the water towards the horse and me. Bandit arched his neck and stretched down. They sniffed each other's noses.

Then the dog turned and splashed back onto the bank. She barked once and ran away down the trail.

"Jackie," I called after the dog.

I gave Bandit a not-so-gentle kick and set off after Jack. I didn't want to lose her. "Come on, Bandit," I whispered. "Let's find Jack!"

We followed her, but I lost sight of the dog as I led Bandit around a curve in the trail.

"Jackie," I called again.

Bandit cantered on. As we rounded the bend, I suddenly had to rein in. "Whoa, Bandit. Whoa, buddy," I called.

Standing in the middle of the trail, blocking the way, were Ben and Midas.

The dog stood at the horse's feet, staring up at Ben. Still grinning, she seemed to be saying, "Look what I found for you," to her master.

"I told you. Her name is Jack," was the first thing Ben had to say.

Relief swept over me at the sight of Ben. "You found us," I cried.

Uncontrollable tears of relief fell from my eyes. I lifted my arm quickly, pretending to wipe away a fly, and wiped the tears off my face. The heavy fabric of the coat was rough against my skin.

"We got lost," I explained unnecessarily. "And before you start yelling at me for leaving the group, I know it was a dumb thing to do, and I'm really sorry."

"So where have you been?" Ben asked. "I've been out looking for you all night." He rubbed his eyes with the back of his hand.

Then I noticed how tired Ben looked. His shoulders slumped, and his eyes were puffy and red. Even Midas hung his head with fatigue. He had lost some of his dazzle. They both looked exhausted.

I had expected Ben to be mad, but he just seemed glad to see me.

"Are you and Bandit okay?" he asked.

I looked down at Bandit and fondly patted his neck. "Bandit's fine," I said. "Hungry, but fine. Me too. I slept under a rock and made an area for Bandit out of baling twine."

"Wow," Ben said, sounding impressed.

"And you were right about the coat, by the way," I admitted. "It did come in handy."

Ben smiled wryly. "So you survived a night alone in the mountains," he said. "That's something very few people can say."

"It's . . . it's beautiful out here," I said. I shifted in my saddle and swallowed.

I wasn't comfortable hearing Ben's words. It almost seemed like he was praising me for surviving the night alone. But I didn't deserve that, and I knew it. Also, I wanted to be honest.

"Well, if I'd been smart and listened to you, instead of trying to prove what a good rider I was, I never would have left the group. Then I would have had a much more comfortable night with other people for company," I muttered.

Ben nodded. "True," was all he said.

Then he dismounted and lifted the flap on his saddlebag. "Come on," he said. "I'll take you back to the house soon, but first you need food. Bandit will have to wait until he's home, but there's a nice big bucket of oats waiting for him when he gets there."

Ben produced a Thermos and a bag of sandwiches.

"You're probably sick of sandwiches," he said as he passed them over. "But it's all I have with me." He took the lid off the thermos, unscrewed the cap, and began pouring dark, steamy hot chocolate into the lid.

I bit into the sandwich. It was turkey, a little squashed and stale, but absolutely delicious after a night without much to eat.

I shook my head. "No way, this is great," I finally said, in between mouthfuls. I took the drink from Ben and gratefully washed down the turkey sandwich with the creamy chocolate drink.

"Compliments of Mum," said Ben, adding, "who is really, really, mad at me, by the way."

"What happened to everyone else?" I asked.

"They're fine," Ben said. "They're back at the house by now, I'm guessing. By the time we realized you were missing yesterday it was too late to do much."

He paused, then added, "I left the satellite phone in the barn when we left on the ride yesterday morning. Mum was not happy about that. When she showed up in the Jeep with the bags, she chewed my ear off. But it was too risky to go back anywhere in the dark."

He shrugged. "Are you ready to go? Did you get enough to eat?" he asked.

"I'm fine," I said. "Let's get going. I want to see Jade as soon as I can."

"Okay," Ben said.

Ben watched me get back on Bandit before mounting Midas. I happily followed Ben's lead as we began the ride back to the house.

His horse walked at a fast pace while Ben and I talked. Bandit stretched out, happy to keep up with Midas.

"So, how is Jade?" I asked. "Did she make it through the rest of the ride?"

"She's worried about you, of course," said Ben. Then he smiled. "And I bet she's more than a little sore. Still, she's done pretty well – considering."

I cringed as a wave of guilt washed over me. I had spoiled everyone's trip. Plus, it had added pressure to Ben's job that he could have done without.

"Is Jade mad at me?" I asked.

Ben didn't say anything for a moment. Then he said, "Jade's upset. She wanted to come looking for you, too, but it was going to be quicker and easier for me to come alone. Actually, you were on the right trail home."

I explained my decision to allow Bandit to find his way home for me.

Ben looked fondly at the grey horse. "He would have taken you there, too," he told me. "He's smart. Bandit was my horse before I got Midas. We've had some really great times together."

"It must be hard letting strangers ride your horses," I said.

"Sometimes," he agreed. "Not everyone understands how to treat them."

"I'd feel weird letting strangers ride my horse, Bobby," I said.

"Well, I guess you're lucky you don't have to," Ben said.

I smiled. "Definitely," I said. "But then again, I haven't had him for long. I guess I'm still pretty new to the horse world."

We rode on in silence a little longer. Then, finally, I said, "I'm sorry I've acted like a stuck-up snob since I got here. I'm not really like that. I swear."

Ben looked away. "Well, I guess I sounded pretty rude and bossy," he admitted. "According to my mum, that's exactly how I am."

I laughed. "Midas is stunning," I said, looking over at the gorgeous golden horse. "I don't think I've ever seen a horse like him. He's so beautiful."

Ben smiled widely and stroked the horse's neck. "He was an orphan foal – I raised him myself." There was no mistaking the pride in Ben's voice.

Suddenly, the trees cleared, and we were back at the Woodland Hills gate. Once we were both through the gate, only a couple of hundred acres of green rolling hills stood between us and the house.

Despite everything, I felt a twinge of disappointment that the ride would soon be over. I wondered if I could save up and come again.

I looked over at Ben and grinned. "Race you back to the house?" I challenged.

Ben's face lit up at my words. "You're on." Ben whooped loudly, and Midas was off.

I held on tight as Bandit charged off after them.

The gallop home was exhilarating. Midas
flew across the field, with Bandit in hot pursuit.
We came thundering over the hill and I saw Jade
standing near the stables. She looked dumbstruck
at the sight of me bent over Bandit's neck at a
flat-out gallop.

The horses' sides heaved. Their bodies were
wet with sweat as Ben and I finally eased them
back to a walk.

Jade didn't wait. As soon as she saw us,
she ran towards me, even though Ben, Midas,

Bandit, and I were still a hundred metres – or more – away from her.

"Annie," Jade screamed out my name. "Are you okay?" Then she yelled, "Who's chasing you?"

Ben and I both burst into laughter at Jade's worried expression. We were both panting almost as heavily as our horses.

"Annie was just . . . showing me . . . that she doesn't always ride so fancy," Ben sputtered between taking in gulps of air.

* * *

Jade wanted to know everything on the train ride back to Ridgeview. I was happy to tell her. I left nothing out, even telling Jade how jealous I'd been of Ben when the two of them had seemed to be shutting me out.

"Oh, Annie, I'm sorry," Jade said. "I was just so nervous. I wanted to stay close to Ben. He was the one who knew where we were going and how the horses might behave."

"And he was cute," I said.

Jade laughed. "Yeah, he was pretty cute," she said, winking at me.

"It's okay," I said. "I get it now. I'm sorry I acted like such an idiot. Ben thinks if we come back next year we can help him herd cattle." I grinned at the thought. "And he even promised me I can ride Midas!"

"I don't know, Annie," Jade said. "Horses are just so big, and they're actually kinda scary. Maybe you should take Reese with you next year."

I looked at my friend. "So much for our weekend away, huh?" I asked. "I hardly saw you." I smiled at her and added, "You know, Jade, you're still my best friend in the city. You always will be."

"And you're still my best friend in the country." Jade wrinkled her nose, thinking. "As a matter of fact," she added, "you're probably my only friend in the country."

We both laughed.

Jade started flipping through a glossy fashion magazine, but I was happy to just gaze out of the window and think.

Jade hadn't changed much since I had moved to the country, but I had changed a lot.

Green fields flashed by the train's window as I daydreamed.

Mrs Cameron had started it all when she gave me Bobby. It seemed so long ago now. At the same time, I had met Reese and the others from riding club.

Then I'd joined riding club and got the job at Erica's stables. I had been to competitions, both as an individual and as part of a team.

"And another thing," Jade said, interrupting my daydream. She was rubbing at her backside as she spoke. "Aren't you sore?" she asked. "Seriously, I had no idea that horse riding would hurt so much."

I laughed. "It only hurts when you're not used to it," I told her. "I was really sore for a while after I first started riding Bobby. Oh, I can't wait to see him."

* * *

My dad and Jade's mother were waiting for us when we arrived at the Willowvale train station. Jade and I waved goodbye to each other.

"I'll call you soon," Jade said.

"You better!" I said. "I'll come visit you in the city as soon as I can."

Once we were in the car, my father wanted to hear all about my night alone with Bandit under the stars.

It turned out that Rita had called him to explain everything.

I listened patiently to his lecture about staying with the group at all times and not putting myself in danger. I knew I deserved it.

Then my dad surprised me by saying, "I'm proud of you. You know, Annie, not too many girls your age would have kept their cool in that situation."

I squirmed in my seat. "Um . . . thanks, Dad," I said.

My father reached out to briefly touch my hand. He smiled. "You'd better let me tell your mother about last night," he said. "I'll break it to her gently."

I shot my father a grateful smile. "Thanks," I said. "That would be great.

When we got home, I said a quick hello to Jonesy and my mother. Then I went straight to

Reese's house. I couldn't wait one more second to bring Bobby home.

"Hey, you. How was it?" Reese called out when she spotted me ducking under our shared fence.

"Great!" I answered brightly.

Reese beckoned me over to a couple of seats and a table on her patio. "Bobby and Jefferson are fine," she said. "Why don't you come and sit for a while? Tell me all about the trip. I want to hear every detail."

I glanced across the paddock to where Bobby and Jefferson were peacefully grazing. My horse didn't look up.

I shrugged. "Okay, why not?" I said. "But I'm warning you, it's a really long story."

"I have time," Reese said. "It's the school holidays, remember?"

I smiled. "Cool," I said. "Oh, and thanks again for that chocolate bar. It was a lifesaver."

Reese looked intrigued. "A lifesaver, huh? Well, there's more inside," she told me. "I'll just go grab some."

I sat down and stared out over the fields. From here, I could see the buildings that made up the township of Ridgeview in the distance.

I was so glad to be home. I sighed – a deep, contented sigh.

Coming to this place had changed my life. I'd left behind old friends but made new ones.

Once, I could never have imagined how much I would come to love the country life and – even more importantly – a life with horses in it.

The door swung open. Reese appeared, holding a tray with two glasses of lemonade and the promised chocolate.

"So, tell me," she demanded, setting the tray down on the table. She leaned forward eagerly.

I took a deep breath. "Reese, you'll never believe it," I began.

About the Author

When she was growing up, Bernadette Kelly desperately wanted her own horse. Although she rode other people's horses, she didn't get one of her own until she was an adult. Many years later, she is still obsessed with horses. Luckily, she lives in the country, where there is plenty of room for her four-legged friends. When she's not writing or working with her horses, Bernadette and her daughter compete at riding club competitions.

Horse Tips from Bernadette

- Make sure that your horse has clean, fresh water at all times.

- Horses need doctors, just like humans do. Make sure your horse is frequently seen by a veterinarian.

- Horses are herd animals. That means they're happier when they're with other horses. Make sure your horse has time to socialize.

- Learn everything you can about horses.

For more, visit Bernadette's website at
www.bernadettekelly.com.au/horses

Glossary

- **boundary** line, fence, or other marking that separates one area from another

- **canter** move at a speed between a gallop and a trot

- **dismount** get off a horse

- **dressage** art of riding and training a horse

- **foal** baby horse

- **girth** part of a horse's saddle that goes under its stomach to secure the saddle

- **jodhpurs** trousers worn for horse riding

- **paddock** enclosed area where horses can graze or exercise

- **Thoroughbred** breed of English horses developed especially for racing

- **unenthusiastic** not excited

- **vault** leap

Dear Annie,

My best friend lives in another city, and I miss her a lot. How can we make sure our friendship stays strong?

Sincerely,

Lonely in Lancaster

Dear Lonely in Lancaster,

Don't worry! Your friend might not live in the same city as you, but that doesn't mean your friendship has to suffer. There are a lot of things you can both do to keep your relationship strong.

Your friendship can live long-distance:

1. **Make an effort.** Go out of your way to call your friend, even if texting or IM is easier. Send real letters. Make plans to video chat so you can talk face to face.

2. **Get creative.** Maybe you won't be at the same school events – but she can still help you pick out outfits using a webcam. Find ways to keep your friendship fun!

3. **Make a date.** Find a way to get together, whether that's once a year or once a week. And make sure you keep your plans.

4. **Be open.** Make sure you don't focus only on this friendship. Your other friends deserve your attention, too!

Any friendship can survive if you take care of it! Good luck!

Love,
♡ Annie

The Ridgeview Book Club Discussion Guide

Use these reading group questions when you and your friends discuss this book:

1. Why did Annie go off on her own during the hike? What would you have done in the same situation? If you were Annie, what would you do when you realized you were lost in the woods?

2. It can be really hurtful when boys get in the way of friendships. What are some ways to deal with this if it happens?

3. When Annie moved to Ridgeview, she left her best friend, Jade, behind in the city. Talk about this. How would you feel if you left your best friend? What would you do to make sure your friendship stayed strong, even if you weren't living in the same place and going to the same school?

The Ridgeview Book Club Journal Prompts

A journal is a private place to record your thoughts and ideas. Use these prompts to get started. If you like, share your writing with your friends.

1. Imagine that you get to go anywhere you want during your school holidays. Where would you go? Plan your dream trip. Don't forget to decide who you'd want to take with you!

2. One of the most difficult things about being a teenager is negotiating your independence. Write about a time when you had to be independent. What happened?

3. When two friends change, their friendships can change, too. Think about your longest friendship. What has made it last so long? Write about the reasons that friendship is important to you.